Spencer
the Express Engine

Based on *The Railway Series* by the Rev. W. Awdry

Illustrations by *Robin Davies and Jerry Smith*

EGMONT

EGMONT

We bring stories to life

First published in Great Britain 2005
This edition published in Great Britain 2013
by Egmont UK Limited
The Yellow Building, 1 Nicholas Road, London W11 4AN

Thomas the Tank Engine & Friends™

CREATED BY BRITT ALLCROFT
Based on the Railway Series by the Reverend W Awdry
© 2013 Gullane (Thomas) LLC. A HIT Entertainment company.
Thomas the Tank Engine & Friends and Thomas & Friends are trademarks of Gullane (Thomas) Limited.
Thomas the Tank Engine & Friends and Design is Reg. U.S. Pat. & Tm. Off.

HiT entertainment

ISBN 978 1 4052 6970 4
43286/23
Printed in Italy

Stay safe online. Egmont is not responsible for content hosted by third parties.

FSC
MIX
Paper
FSC® C018306

Egmont is passionate about helping to preserve the world's remaining ancient forests.
We only use paper from legal and sustainable forest sources.

This book is made from paper certified by the Forest Stewardship Council® (FSC®),
an organisation dedicated to promoting responsible management of forest resources.
For more information on the FSC, please visit www.fsc.org. To learn more about
Egmont's sustainable paper policy, please visit www.egmont.co.uk/ethical

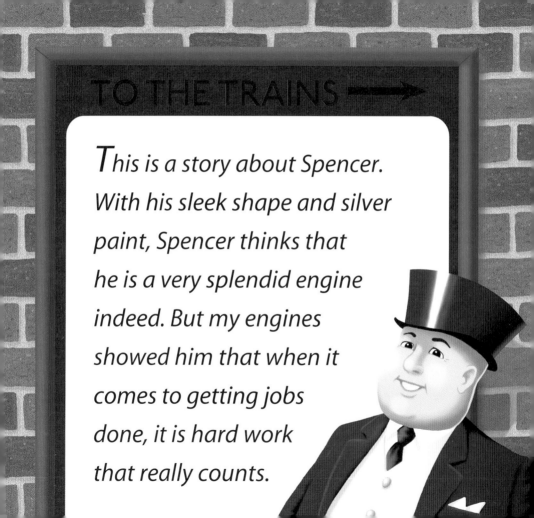

This is a story about Spencer. With his sleek shape and silver paint, Spencer thinks that he is a very splendid engine indeed. But my engines showed him that when it comes to getting jobs done, it is hard work that really counts.

One day, the Duke and Duchess came to Sodor for a visit. Gordon hoped that he would have the special job of showing the important visitors around the Island.

But, to Gordon's disappointment, the Duke and Duchess brought their own engine with them. His name was Spencer, and he was the shiniest, sleekest engine that Gordon had ever seen.

That afternoon, there was to be a party at Maron Station for the Duke and Duchess.

 "That's on the other side of Gordon's Hill," James told Spencer.

"You'll need to take on plenty of water," Gordon added, helpfully.

"I have plenty of water," wheeshed Spencer, as he steamed out of the yard.

But when Spencer reached Gordon's Hill, he began to struggle. The hill was long and steep. He puffed. He panted. He pulled with all his might. But Spencer had run out of steam.

His Driver had to phone for help.

Back at the station, the Station Master told Gordon, "The Fat Controller has a job for you. There's an engine stuck on a hill."

Gordon set off at once.

Gordon was surprised to find Spencer.

"What's wrong?" he asked.

"No water!" snapped Spencer. "I must have a leaky tank."

"Perhaps," smiled Gordon. "But we'd better hurry. Everyone is waiting for the Duke and Duchess."

Soon, Gordon was coupled up to Spencer, and they set off.

Minutes later, they arrived at Maron Station. The party was ready to begin.

"Well done, Gordon," said The Fat Controller. "You are a Very Useful Engine!"

Gordon glowed with pride.

Spencer was a very fast engine. One day, when he pulled into Knapford Station, his Driver had exciting news for him.

"You have beaten Gordon's record," he said.

"Of course," boasted Spencer. "I'm faster and finer than all the engines on Sodor put together."

The Fat Controller's engines were very cross.

Spencer was taking the Duke and Duchess to their summer house. The Fat Controller came to tell his engines that one of them was needed to carry their furniture. The engines saw the chance for a race!

"Please, Sir!" said Thomas, James and Gordon all together. "May I go?"

But The Fat Controller told Edward to go instead.

James and Gordon groaned. Edward was an old engine, and not as strong and fast as the others.

"He'll lose the race and let the whole Railway down!" said James.

Thomas and Percy were cross with James. Edward was their friend.

"You can beat that big, silver show-off any day!" they told him.

Slowly and steadily, Edward set off.

"Will-do-my-best, will-do-my-best," he puffed.

But Spencer quickly passed Edward.

"I've won already," he boasted.

And with a whoosh, he was gone!

Edward came to the bottom of a steep hill. The furniture was heavy and he felt tired.

But Donald and Douglas were waiting at the junction. They had heard about the race.

"Hoorah for Edward!" cried Donald.

"He's a first rate engine!" added Douglas.

This made Edward feel much better. He huffed and puffed and soon he had climbed to the top of the hill. He raced down the other side to catch up with Spencer.

Spencer happily steamed along. Up ahead was the siding leading to the summer house.

But the Duke wanted to take some photographs of the countryside. Spencer stopped, and the Duke set up his camera.

Spencer closed his eyes. "Nothing to worry about," he said, lazily.

Before long, Spencer was fast asleep.

When the Duke had finished taking photographs, Spencer's Driver rang the bell.

"Time to go," he said.

Nothing happened.

Spencer was dreaming of winning the race. He didn't hear the bell. And he didn't hear Edward puffing past him. Spencer's Driver rang the bell again and again.

Finally, Spencer opened his eyes. He couldn't believe what he saw. Edward was heading towards the summer house.

"Nearly-there-nearly-there," gasped the old engine.

Spencer took off as fast as he could, but he was too late.

Edward pulled to a stop in front of the summer house.

"I've won," he gasped. "I did it!"

Suddenly his pistons didn't ache and his axles weren't shaking. Edward felt like the pride of the Sodor Railway.

And he was right.